THIS BOOK BELONGS TO

This edition published by HarperCollins Publishers Ltd 1999 for Silverdale Books
An imprint of Bookmart Ltd
Registered Number 2372865
Trading as Bookmart Limited
Desford Rd, Enderby, Leicester, LE9 5AD
First published 1956 by Sampson Lowe
© Darrell Waters Limited 1956 as to all text and illustrations
Enid Blyton's signature mark and the word 'NODDY' are Registered
Trade Marks of Enid Blyton Ltd
All rights reserved
ISBN 0 26 167246-0
Printed and bound in Italy

BE BRAVE LITTLE NODDY!

BY Enid Blyton

CONTENTS

1. Round the Corner
2. Mr Honk
3. Be Brave, Little Noddy!
4. Noddy Finds Some Work
5. A Dreadful Shock
6. Good News!
7. Parp-parp-parp!
8. Honk! Honk!
9. Big-Ears is Very Clever

NODDY FOUND HIMSELF SITTING ON A PILE OF
ORANGES AND TOMATOES

10

of his car, high into the air—and landed on Sid Cat's fruit barrow nearby.

Plonk! Noddy found himself sitting on a pile of oranges and tomatoes—and, dear me, quite a lot of them had fallen off the barrow and were rolling in the road!

"Oh, what's happened?" wailed Noddy. "Who's been silly enough to leave their car so near the corner?"

It wasn't long before quite a crowd collected round. Sid Cat was very cross about his oranges and tomatoes—and someone else was looking very angry too.

It was the man who owned the car. He was a wooden man, but bigger than Noddy, and he wore a bright yellow coat and blue trousers, and had a feather in his red hat.

"Now then!" he shouted, shaking his fist at little Noddy. "What's all this?"

2. MR HONK

Noddy went to look at his own little car. "Oh, it's hurt!" he cried. "Look, the bonnet is broken— and one of the lamps is smashed. Oh, little car, do you feel all right?"

"Poooop," said the car, in a very small voice.

"Can't you say 'Parp-parp', little car?" asked Noddy anxiously, and pressed the hooter. It was no good—it could only say a very soft "Pooooop!"

"Who cares about your silly car!" said the angry man. "You might have smashed mine to bits. I'll report you!"

"Now then, now then," said a very deep voice, and up came Mr Plod the policeman, taking out his notebook as he came. "What's happening here?"

"Ha—Mr Plod!" said the angry man. "I'm Mr Honk from Toy-Car Town. I parked my car just over there and round the corner came this red and yellow car, at sixty miles an hour . . ."

"I didn't, I didn't, I didn't!" cried Noddy. "Oooh, what a storyteller! Mr Plod, I . . ."

"Now, now—one at a time," said Mr Plod. "Mr Honk—what damage is done to your car?"

"I DIDN'T damage his car!" said Noddy, his head nodding up and down so fast that it was quite

difficult to see it. "It's such a big car, look—and mine's a little one. *My* car is the one that got hurt."

"WILL you be quiet, Noddy!" said Mr Plod. "I'm talking to Mr Honk.

13

Mr Honk—if any damage is done to your car Noddy
will have to pay for it."

"I should think so!" said Mr Honk, still looking
very fierce.

"But, Mr Plod—how could I know that Mr Honk

had parked his car *just* round the corner?" wept
Noddy, very upset to see his car so hurt. "You *know*
it's not right to do that, you know it isn't."

"Noddy's right!" called a voice. It was Miss Fluffy

14

Cat. "No one should park a car right on a corner."

"Well," said Mr Plod, "well, perhaps, Mr Honk, it would have been better if you . . ."

"Now don't you bother about this, Mr Plod," said Mr Honk, hurriedly. "I don't want Noddy to be punished. We'll say no more about it. In fact I'll tow Noddy's car to the garage. I can't say fairer than that."

"Well," said Mr Plod again, "I suppose that's all right. After all your car *hasn't* been damaged—but it *would* have been better if you had parked . . ."

"Yes, yes, yes," said Mr Honk, getting into his car. "Noddy, have you a rope? Tie your car on to mine and I'll give you a tow."

Noddy was surprised that the angry Mr Honk was now being so kind. He didn't know that Mr Honk was afraid that Mr Plod was changing his

15

mind about the accident and might be going to blame *him* for it.

Poor Noddy found a rope and tied the front of his little car to the back of Mr Honk's big shiny one. "Poooooop!" said the little car, softly and sadly. Noddy patted its bonnet, and felt sad too.

Then he got into the car, and took the steering-wheel. "I'm ready!" he called to Mr Honk, and off they went, Noddy's car wobbling as it ran along behind.

They came to the garage and Mr Honk got out. "What are you?" he asked Noddy. "A taxi-driver?"

"Yes," said Noddy, his head nodding fast.

"I shouldn't think you earn much money, taking passengers in that silly little car," said Mr Honk. "Now a car like mine—big, shiny, fast—*that's* the kind to have!"

16

NODDY'S CAR WOBBLED ALONG BEHIND
MR HONK'S BIG SHINY CAR

17

"Big-Ears — oh, Big-Ears!" said Noddy, trying to find his hanky. "Oh, Big-Ears!"

"Good gracious — what *has* happened?" said Big-Ears. "Come in and tell me!"

And soon Noddy was pouring out all that had happened. Big-Ears listened in surprise.

"Well, well—what bad luck, Noddy!" he said. "Still, it might have been worse. You might have been badly hurt, and Sid Cat might have made you pay for his fruit. Mr Plod might even have put you in prison. Cheer up!"

"I can't cheer up," said Noddy.

"Yes you can," said Big-Ears. "You're going to have some fun finding all kinds of new jobs to do till your car is mended, and you're going to show everyone how brave you are, and how you can laugh when things go wrong!"

"Am I?" said Noddy.

"Of course you are!" said Big-Ears. "Now, let's make up a Brave Song—you're good at making up songs, Noddy. Think of a really nice Brave Song."

"I can't," said Noddy, his head nodding sadly. "You're going to be disappointed in me, Big-Ears. I don't feel very brave about this. I keep remembering my poor little car and how it can only say 'Poooooop!' instead of 'Parp-parp!' Oh, Big-Ears—it did sound sad!"

Big-Ears didn't take any notice of all this. He began beating time with his right hand and singing.

"De-dee, de-dee, de-dee-dee-dee," he sang, to Noddy's astonishment. "Now let me see—how would a Brave Song go?

"Oh, what does it matter if things go wrong,
    I'll sing and I'll whistle . . .
Dear, dear, I'm not at all good at making up songs."

"I know how that ought to go," said Noddy,

21

cheering up. "Like this, Big-Ears—you just listen."
And he nodded his head and sang:

"Oh, what does it matter
If things go wrong,
I'll sing and I'll whistle
The whole day long.
I'll go on smiling,
I'll laugh, ho ho!
And brave as a soldier
You'll see me go.
My head is a-nodding,
My little bell rings,
My feet are a-dancing
As if they had wings.
Oh, WHAT DOES IT MATTER
If things go wrong,
I'll sing and I'll whistle
My Brave Little Song!"

Noddy sang this very
loudly in his little
high voice, and he
danced all round Big-
Ears as he sang,
nodding his head till
his bell jingled merrily.

NODDY SANG VERY LOUDLY IN HIS LITTLE
HIGH VOICE

23

Big-Ears clapped and clapped when Noddy had finished. "Well done!" he said. "The best song you've ever thought of, little Noddy. Why, look— you've even made my old cat dance!"

"Oh, Cat—come and dance with *me*," said Noddy. "Big-Ears and I will sing the Brave Song again, and you can meow. Give me your front paws, Cat."

And there was little Noddy dancing round with the big old cat and singing away at the top of his voice. "Really," Big-Ears said, "it's enough to make a cat laugh." And certainly *his* cat was smiling all over its whiskery face!

"I feel better now, Big-Ears," said Noddy, sitting down to get his breath. "That's a good song, isn't it? I'll sing it whenever I feel sad."

"That's right," said Big-Ears. "Face up to trouble, little Noddy, and it will run away—but if *you* run away, trouble will come after you. Now—let's make plans."

4. NODDY FINDS SOME WORK

BIG-EARS was a very, very good friend. He got out a plate of cakes, and a bottle of raspberry syrup made from his own raspberries. Noddy beamed all over his face.

"This makes me feel better too," he said, taking a cake. "Now—what other job shall I do, Big-Ears, till my car is mended?"

"I'll lend you my bicycle," said Big-Ears, "and we'll tie a little wooden cart behind it, Noddy— and you can deliver all kinds of things for the people in Toy Town."

"Oh, Big-Ears—what a very good idea!" said Noddy, munching his cake. "I shall like that. Will you *really* lend me your bicycle? What will you do without it?"

"I'll manage," said Big-Ears, and his face looked so kind that Noddy got up and gave him a big hug.

"I'll give you half the money I earn," said Noddy, his head nodding hard. "And I'll keep your bicycle as clean as I can."

"Let's go and get it now," said Big-Ears. "Dear me, surely you don't want *another* cake, Noddy— that's your fourth."

"Oh dear—you're too good at counting, Big-Ears," said Noddy. "Yes—let's get your bicycle."

Well, it wasn't long before Noddy was riding merrily through the wood on Big-Ears' bicycle. When two small rabbits got in his way he rang the bicycle bell and then he felt sad because it said "R-r-r-r-ring, r-r-r-r-ring!" instead of "Parp-parp!" as his little hooter did.

"Now, now—I must remember my Brave Song," said Noddy to himself, and he sang it in time to his pedalling.

"Oh, what does it matter
    If things go wrong,
I'll sing and I'll whistle
    The whole day long!"

People were most surprised to see Noddy on Big-Ears' bicycle, but when he explained that the little cart was for carrying things until his car was mended, they were all very kind.

Mrs Tubby Bear was the first to give him a job. "Look," she said, "I've just finished doing some washing for old Miss Skittle. Take it in your little cart for me, Noddy. She will give you some money and you can keep sixpence of it for yourself."

"Oh, thank you, Mrs Tubby Bear!" said Noddy, very pleased. He put the basket into the little cart, got on the bicycle, and away he went. It was rather hard work pedalling up the hill to Miss Skittle's house, but never mind—he had his Brave Song to sing!

"I mustn't forget that," said Noddy to himself. "I still keep feeling sad, so I must sing the Brave Song as often as I can. And this evening I'll go and see my little car and sing it the Brave Song to cheer it up, because I expect it's feeling rather sad too."

27

The car was very glad when Noddy rode into the garage on Big-Ears' bicycle. "Pooooooooop!" it said, and jiggled up and down a little. Noddy patted its bonnet and then he danced round it and sang the Brave Song. The car joined in with a few little "Pooooooooops".

Mr Sparks smiled at Noddy. "I'm doing my best to mend your car quickly," he said. "I'm glad to see you're being so brave about it, Noddy."

"Big-Ears made me brave," said Noddy. "I'm not *really* a very brave person, Mr Sparks. I could easily burst into tears when I think about my poor little car—look, this lamp is quite smashed. Oh dear!"

"Off you go!" said Mr Sparks. "Unless you want

me to use your tears to wash down this car. It would save me getting out the hose! Come and cry over this muddy car bonnet and make it nice and wet."

"Now you've made me laugh!" said little Noddy, and he nodded his head and smiled. "Goodbye, Mr Sparks. Goodbye, car. I'll come again."

28

NODDY DANCED AROUND THE CAR AND
SANG THE BRAVE SONG

29

"Pooooooop!" said the little car, in its new, soft little voice.

Noddy hurried out with Big-Ears' bicycle. "Now—who wants something delivering?" he wondered, and he rang the bell and sang loudly:

"Hallo, hallo,
Does anybody
Want some help
From little Noddy?
Parcels carried
Here and there,
Shopping fetched
From anywhere!"

5. A DREADFUL SHOCK

NEXT day Noddy cleaned Big-Ears' bicycle
before he set out with the little cart behind.

"Bicycle, I'll clean you well,
Handle-bars and wheels and bell,
Then I'll pedal you away
And earn my living all the day!"

sang Noddy as he polished and rubbed. Mrs Tubby
Bear heard him and looked over the wall.

"You're a good little Noddy," she said. "Why
don't you go to the Noah's Ark this morning and ask
Mrs Noah if you can do her shopping for her? It's
her busy day today. She could give you her shopping list and you could bring everything back to the
Ark in that little cart."

"Oh, what a good idea!" said Noddy, and jumped on to the bicycle at once. Away he went, with the little cart trailing behind.

Mrs Noah was very pleased to see him. It was her washing day and little Noddy could hardly see her, there were so many soapy bubbles in the washing-tub.

"If you've got your shopping list, I'll go to the shops for you and bring everything back," said Noddy, nodding his head.

"Well, well—to think you've got Big-Ears' bicycle and little cart!" said Mrs Noah. "And you're getting all kinds of jobs till your little car is mended, I hear. You're a good, brave little Noddy, because we all know it wasn't *your* fault that your car was damaged!"

"No, it wasn't," said Noddy. "It was Mr Honk's fault—and he didn't even say he was sorry. But never mind, it will soon be mended and then I can be your taxi-driver again!"

Noddy took Mrs Noah's list and set off. He didn't see that one of the Noah's Ark monkeys had leapt into the little cart behind—look what a fine time he's having!

"Dear me—this cart's very heavy all of a sudden!" said Noddy, panting. Then he looked round. "Oh—you bad monkey! I'll take you straight to Mr Plod!"

But the monkey jumped out at once, and leapt up to the roof of a house so Noddy couldn't get him. Noddy pedalled on. Suddenly he saw a big shiny car coming down the middle of the road. It swept by and almost knocked Noddy into the gutter.

On the front of the car was a notice—and what *do* you think it said? It said:

TAXI FOR HIRE
SIXPENCE A
TIME

Noddy couldn't believe his eyes! He got off the bicycle and stared after the car. He knew that car—and he knew the driver!

"Why—that was Mr Honk!" said Noddy. "Good gracious me! MR HONK! And he's using his car as a taxi—in Toy Town too, where *I'm* the taxi-driver!"

The big shiny car stopped and picked up the Sailor Doll and his wife and little boy. It was such a big car that it could easily take them all. Then off it went again, and Noddy could hear it hooting proudly.

"Honk! Honk! Honk!"

Suddenly Noddy wasn't brave any more. He sat down on the kerb by the gutter and wailed loudly, the tears splashing round his feet.

"It's Mr Honk! He made me have an accident  because he parked his car near a corner—and now while my car's being mended *he's* being a taxi-driver! And his car is MUCH bigger; he'll take all my passengers and I'll NEVER be a taxi-driver again!"

THE BIG SHINY CAR PICKED UP THE SAILOR DOLL AND HIS
WIFE AND LITTLE BOY

35

Just at that moment Mrs Tubby Bear came by—and she was most surprised to see Noddy sitting on the kerb with tears rolling down his cheeks.

"Why, little Noddy—I thought you were so brave!" she said. "Surely you're not crying about your little car!"

"I'm c-c-crying because Mr Honk is using his c-c-car as a t-t-taxi," wept Noddy. "And I'M the taxi-d-d-driver here."

"Get up, Noddy," said Mrs Tubby Bear. "Don't worry about Mr Honk. As soon as your car is mended everyone will want you to drive them again—and no-one will want Mr Honk."

"Won't they?" said Noddy, standing up, his head nodding sadly. "They might! His car is bigger than mine and it goes very fast."

"Let me wipe your eyes," said Mrs Tubby Bear. "Now—what about that Brave Song you sang to me yesterday? Get on Big-Ears' bicycle and ride away singing it. Go along. Come to tea this afternoon and have some of my strawberry jam."

Noddy tried to smile. He got on his bicycle and rode away slowly, trying to sing his Brave Song.

"Oh, what does it matter (sniff-sniff-SNIFF)
When things go wrong (oh dear, oh dear!)
I'll sing and I'll whistle
The whole day long! (sniff-sniff-SNIFF!)"

But by the time he had got to the end of the song he felt much better, and rang his bell so fiercely at Mr Wobbly Man that he wobbled into the middle of a very big puddle and got stuck there.

"That horrid Mr Honk," said Noddy, as he cycled off to do Mrs Noah's shopping. "Mean Mr Honk! I don't LIKE Mr Honk! But oh dear — I expect he's a very, very good taxi-driver!"

6. GOOD NEWS!

NODDY was very busy that day and the next. He
did the shopping for a great many people and
trundled it home for them in the little cart, which
quite enjoyed itself jolting and jiggling up and
down the road behind Noddy.

"I take your parcel
   And your bundle
   And my little cart I trundle!" sang Noddy.
"And I'll quickly
   Do your shopping—
   See me cycle without stopping!
   I am trusty,
   Safe and steady,
   Always quick and always ready!"

"Have you heard Noddy's new little song?" said Miss Fluffy Cat to Mr Monkey. "Really, he's a good little fellow, you know—and very brave about the accident to his little car."

"Yes. He took all my potatoes to market for me and never dropped one," said Mr Monkey. "*And* he stood there and sold them for me. By the way—have you seen Mr Honk's taxi? It's very grand indeed."

"Yes, I've seen it," said Miss Fluffy Cat. "Well, I shall use it till Noddy's car comes back from the garage, but after that I shall have Noddy again. We shan't want Mr Honk then."

"No, of course we shan't," said Mr Monkey. "He'll have to go somewhere else then. We don't need *two* taxi-drivers in Toy Town."

Noddy went to see his little car quite often, and it always said "Pooooooop" as soon as he walked into the garage. But one evening it said "Parp-parp" in its old voice, and Noddy jumped for joy.

"Oh! You can say 'Parp-parp' again, little car,"

39

he said. "Are you feeling better?"

"Parp-parp-PARP!" said the little car and jiggled up and down on its four wheels.

"Your bonnet's mended," said Noddy, "and you have a new lamp. You want some new paint, then you'll be ready for me to drive again!"

"I'm going to paint your car this evening," said Mr Sparks. "It will be ready tomorrow—but there's rather a big bill to pay, Noddy."

"You can have half the money I've been earning with Big-Ears' bicycle and little cart," said Noddy, happily. "And if that's not enough I'll soon earn some more."

"If Mr Honk stays on here in Toy Town you won't earn very much," said Mr Sparks.

"Oh, but he's sure to go as soon as my car's mended again!" said Noddy. "I do feel happy to think I'll soon drive my little car once more. Aren't *you* happy, little car?"

"I'M GOING TO PAINT YOUR CAR THIS EVENING,"
SAID MR SPARKS

"Parp-parp-PARP!" said the little car, and jiggled again.

"Well, goodbye now," said Noddy. "I'll come and fetch you tomorrow, little car. I'll take Big-Ears' bicycle and cart back to him now, and stay the night with him—and then fetch you tomorrow morning."

And off he went for the last time on Big-Ears' bicycle, with the little cart trundling merrily after him. He came to Big-Ears' Toadstool House and rang the bicycle bell loudly.

"Big-Ears, Big-Ears!" he cried. "I've good news! Open the door quickly and let me in!"

7. PARP-PARP-PARP!

BIG-EARS was very pleased to hear all that Noddy had to say. He was glad to see Noddy so happy and to hear his bell tinkling cheerfully too.

"This evening I'm going to clean your bicycle very, very well for the last time, Big-Ears," said Noddy. "And then I shall count out half my money for you for lending it to me. You are a good friend to me, Big-Ears, thank you very much."

"Well, you've been very brave about everything, little Noddy," said Big-Ears, pleased. "Especially when you saw that horrid Mr Honk taking your place as a taxi-driver in Toy Town. That was a mean thing to do. People don't like him very much, you know."

"Why don't they?" asked Noddy, in surprise.

"He drives much too fast and he won't always carry people's bags for them," said Big-Ears. "And he isn't very polite. Ah well—he won't be here much longer. You'll be our taxi-driver tomorrow."

Noddy cleaned Big-Ears' bicycle and the little cart too. Then he counted out half the money he had earned and gave it to Big-Ears, and put the other half away for Mr Sparks at the garage.

"It's getting late, Noddy," said Big-Ears. "Time you were in bed."

"I'll set the alarm clock for seven o'clock," said Noddy, sleepily. "Then I shall be able to go and fetch my car as soon as the garage opens. Good night, Big-Ears. What about the cat? It's right in the middle of my bed and it won't move."

Big-Ears made a squeak just like a mouse, and you should have seen the cat leap off at once and go sniffing into the corners. That made

45

Noddy laugh and his little bell ring.

"You are so clever, Big-Ears," he said. "Cat, don't you dare jump on me when I'm asleep! See you tomorrow morning at seven o'clock, Big-Ears!"

But Noddy heard something else before the alarm went off at seven o'clock! At just five minutes to seven something ran right up to the front door of Big-Ears' house—and then there came a sound that Noddy knew very well indeed!

"Parp. Parp-parp-PARP!"

Noddy woke up with a jump and leapt out of bed, shouting, "It's my little car! It wouldn't wait for me to fetch it. It's come to find me!"

And sure enough it *was* his little car! It had shot out of the garage as soon as Mr Sparks had opened the doors, and had gone all the way to the Toadstool House by itself.

"IT'S MY LITTLE CAR!" SHOUTED NODDY. "IT'S COME
TO FIND ME!"

47

Noddy ran out and jumped into the driver's seat. He drove up and down the woodland path, hooting madly, and all the little rabbits peeped out to see whatever could be happening!

"It's Noddy and his car," they told one another. "He's got his car again. Listen!"

"Parp-parp-parp-parpparp!" Yes, everyone knew that Noddy had his little car again and would soon be going into Toy Town to pick up passengers as usual.

8. HONK! HONK!

BIG-EARS and Noddy had a very quick breakfast and then they drove down to the village to show everyone that Noddy had his car back. Mrs Tubby Bear was very pleased when he stopped and hooted outside her house.

"Oh—there's Noddy and his car again!" she said to Mr Tubby Bear. "We must get him to take us to the station this morning to meet your brother."

She called out of the window to tell Noddy. Noddy's head nodded happily.

"Yes, yes—I'll fetch you in plenty of time," he said. "I'm just taking Mr Toy Dog to the barber's to have his whiskers cut."

"Parp-parp-parp!" Everyone was pleased to hear that sound again. Noddy was very happy indeed. After dropping Big-Ears at House-For-One, he took Mr Toy Dog to the barber and then he went to fetch the Tubby Bears to take them to the station.

Mrs Tubby Bear couldn't find her purse, so they were rather late in starting—and oh, what a DREADFUL shock Noddy had when they reached the station!

Mr Honk was there in his big, shiny car—and he had got Mr Tubby Bear's brother in the passenger seat, and was driving him out of the station yard to Mr Tubby's House.

"Hey!" cried Noddy, indignantly. "What are you doing, taking passengers when *I'm* back again, Mr Honk? How dare you! I'm the taxi-driver in this town."

"Honk, honk!" hooted Mr Honk's car and swept so near Noddy's that Noddy had to wrench his

wheel round to get out of the way.

"Ha ha, ho ho!" laughed Mr Honk. "*I'm* the taxi-driver now, Noddy—and you can't do anything about it!" And away he went with Tubby Bear's brother.

"What a horrid fellow!" said Mrs Tubby Bear. "Oh, Noddy—I do so hope he won't stay here. He'll be meeting all the trains and taking your passengers."

Noddy was most alarmed. Nobody could make Mr Honk go away if he wanted to stay, that was

certain. Not even Mr Plod the policeman.

Noddy began to wail. "His car is bigger than mine! It takes more passengers. It goes faster. Whatever am I to do?"

"Now, now, Noddy, don't wail like that," said Mr Tubby Bear. "Let's go back to your house and ask Big-Ears what to do—you left him there this morning, didn't you?"

"Yes, I did," said Noddy. "We'll go back to him. Oh dear—Mr Honk will be just outside your house, Mr Tubby Bear, because he's taken your brother there, and he'll hoot at me again."

Off they went to Noddy's house and found Big-Ears standing in the front garden looking in surprise at Mr Honk's car. Mr Honk had just gone indoors with Tubby Bear's brother, carrying some of his luggage and hoping for a good tip.

"Big-Ears, Big-Ears, Mr Honk says he won't go away!" shouted Noddy, almost tumbling out of his car. "What shall I do? Oh, I'm so miserable!"

"Now then—what about your Brave Song?" said Big-Ears, looking quite stern. "Go indoors, Noddy, and sing it at the top of your voice—and then come out here. I promise you that everything will be quite all right then."

"Oh, Big-Ears—whatever do you mean?" said Noddy in surprise. He went into his little House-For-One and shut the door. He stood in the middle of the floor and sang loudly:

"NOW THEN—WHAT ABOUT YOUR BRAVE SONG?"
SAID BIG-EARS TO NODDY QUITE STERNLY

53

"Oh, what does it matter
If things go wrong,
I'll sing and I'll whistle
The whole day long!
(Can I come out now, Big-Ears? No? All right, I'll
sing again.)

I'll go on smiling
I'll laugh, ho ho!
And brave as a soldier
You'll see me go.
My head is a-nodding,
My little bell rings,
My feet are a-dancing
As if they had wings.
Oh, WHAT DOES IT MATTER
If things go wrong,
I'll sing and I'll whistle
My Brave Little Song!"

9. BIG-EARS IS VERY CLEVER

THEN out marched Noddy bravely with a smile on his face. "Did you hear me?" he asked. "I feel better again now. What have you been doing, Big-Ears? You said you'd make everything all right."

"Ssh!" said Big-Ears, as Mr Honk came striding out of Mr Tubby Bear's house next door, jingling some money. He grinned rudely at Noddy.

"You may as well give up!" he said. "I tell you, *I'm* the taxi-driver now! Who wants to ride in your silly little car when they can hire my lovely big shiny one?"

"It's a horrid car!" shouted Noddy. "A tinny one — just a clockwork one!"

Mr Honk got into his car and hooted his horn

loudly to drown what Noddy was saying. Then he
drove off, and Noddy watched him go, feeling very
sad. He turned to Big-Ears.

"But, Big-Ears," he said, in rather a wobbly voice,
"you said—you did say—you'd make things all
right! And you haven't!"

"Oh, haven't I?" said Big-Ears, with the biggest
smile Noddy had ever seen on his face before.
"Well—look here!"

And Big-Ears held out his hand—and in it was a
big clockwork key! Yes—the key to Mr Honk's
car!

"Ooooh! BIG-EARS! Why—it's the key of that clockwork car!" cried Noddy. "Ooooh! When the car runs down he won't be able to wind it up again—so it won't go."

"It certainly won't!" said Big-Ears, beaming. "It serves him right. Damaging your car—and taking your job—and being so rude as well! I won't have it!"

"Oh, Big-Ears—but what will he *say*?" cried Noddy, his eyes shining. "He'll guess it's you."

"Yes—of course," said Big-Ears. "And he'll come back and demand his key—and he shall have it too, *if* he promises to go right away and never come back!"

"Big-Ears, you are the cleverest person I know!" said Noddy, and he gave him such a hug that Big-Ears quite lost his breath. "Oh, Big-Ears, whatever should I do without you? Quick—let's go to the ice-cream shop and see if it's open. Come on, little car—I like your parp-parp much better than that horrid honk-honk!"

And away they went together, with Noddy singing loudly:

AWAY WENT NODDY AND BIG-EARS TOGETHER, WITH
NODDY SINGING LOUDLY

59

"Oh what does it matter
If things go wrong,
I've only to wait
Till my friend comes along.
(Parp-parp-parp!)
He's kind and he's clever,
His name you all know,
And this song is to tell you
That I love him so!
(Parp-parp-parp!)"

"Look—look!" said Big-Ears, pointing ahead. "Mr Honk's car has run down already. Oh, Noddy—*now* we're going to have some fun!"

And so they are—but really I don't feel a BIT sorry for that horrid Mr Honk, do you?